underwater pirates

TIDE STEALERS

THE SUNKEN KINGDOM 2

TIDE STEALERS

by Kim Wilkins

illustrated by D. M. Cornish

Random House New York

Text copyright © 2006 by Kim Wilkins
Illustrations copyright © 2006 by D. M. Cornish

All rights reserved.
Published in the United States by Random House Children's Books,
a division of Random House, Inc., New York. Originally published
in Australia by Omnibus Books, an imprint
of Scholastic Australia Pty. Ltd., Gosford, in 2006.

Random House and colophon are registered trademarks of
Random House, Inc.

Visit us on the Web!
www.randomhouse.com/kids

Educators and librarians, for a variety of teaching tools, visit us at
www.randomhouse.com/teachers

Library of Congress Cataloging-in-Publication Data
Wilkins, Kim.
Tide stealers / Kim Wilkins ;
illustrated by D. M. Cornish. — 1st ed.
p.   cm. — (The sunken kingdom ; bk. 2)
Summary: When underwater pirates steal Asa's Moonstone Star, she and
her brother Rollo search for it across their vast, flooded kingdom, and
along the way face ghosts, sea giants, and secrets about their own past.
ISBN 978-0-375-84807-0 (trade) —
ISBN 978-0-375-94807-7 (lib. bdg.)
[1. Brothers and sisters—Fiction. 2. Fantasy.] I. Cornish, D. M. (David
M.), ill. II. Title.
PZ7.W64867Tid 2008
[Fic]—dc22   2007033804

MANUFACTURED IN MALAYSIA
10 9 8 7 6 5 4 3 2 1
First Edition
Random House Children's Books supports the First Amendment and
celebrates the right to read.

For Luka

CONTENTS

CHAPTER 1

THE STAR IN
THE POOL

It had been a long time since Asa had seen magic.

Down by the edge of the inlet, she held the Moonstone Star in the fingers of her left hand. She knelt and dipped it slowly in the water. Suddenly it was alive with rainbow colors, with swirls of glittering light. She smiled, then checked behind her guiltily. If her aunt Katla or her younger brother, Rollo, saw her down here, dunking her family's most treasured possession in the water, she could be in a lot of trouble.

Asa turned back to the Star and watched the magic pour off it. Her mother, the Star Queen, had told her that the magic was activated by the water of the great oceans. Once, her mother and father had ruled the entire Star Lands, before the evil magician Flood had killed them and taken over. With her mother dead, Asa should have been the new Star Queen. But she and her brother and baby sister were in hiding, fearful of Flood's spies.

"All right, Star," she said softly. "Let's try a little magic." She closed her eyes, as she had seen her mother do when saying spells, but she didn't really know what to do next. So she took a deep breath and said, "Make a fish come to the surface."

Asa opened her eyes and scanned the water. No fish. A big sigh. Maybe she had to be older, or have some kind of training before she could do magic. It was disappointing. She watched the Star a little longer, then pulled it from the water. The sun was hiding behind clouds today and the smell of salt on the air was heavy. She could hear a distant ripple and saw, out in the inlet, a slow stream of bubbles.

Her fish! It had to be! The magic was working after all. Asa dropped the Star in the water again. "Come on, little fishy," she said. All was still, and for a moment she thought that nothing was going to happen—

Sssssssssshhh!

The water split open four feet in front of her and a longship heaved out! It was wooden, black with algae. Water poured off its bow, seaweed streamed behind it. This was no little fish: this was a band of tide stealers. Asa screamed and jumped backward. Seventeen men were crowded onto the boat. Their faces were dark, their teeth crooked, their clothes wet. They wore helmets with yellowed horns set into them. Four of the men were rapidly bailing water out of the ship. The leader, a brawny man with a circlet of gold on his head, pointed to the Star.

"Give it to me!" he shouted.

"No!" Asa turned to run. Behind her, she could hear men diving into the water. Her heart thundered.

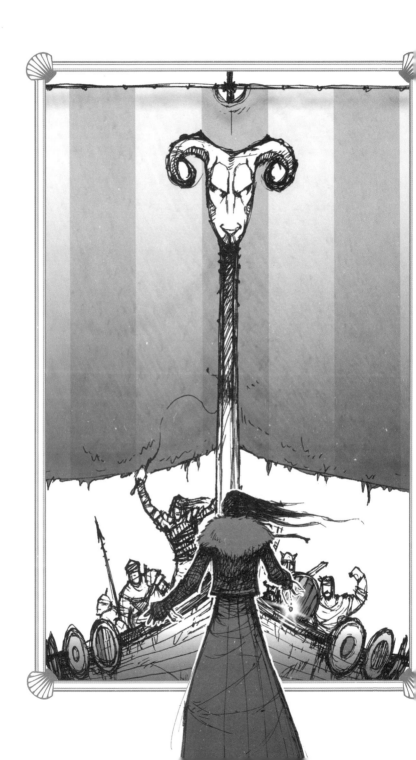

Footsteps were gaining on her. Then a loud crack sounded through the air. She glanced around to see that their leader had whipped out a glistening silver rope. It cut across her hand, catching the Moonstone Star in its cruel tip and jerking it back to where he stood.

"Give it back!" she shouted, turning.

The tide stealers were pouring back onto the boat.

"Give it back!" She ran boldly to the edge of the shore, but her voice was drowned out by the sound of the longship submerging again. Water rushed in to fill the gap; bubbles spewed upward in streams. It all happened in moments.

Then silence. Asa could hear her own breathing, loud in her ears.

"No, no," she whispered.

The Moonstone Star, her family's magic, the last memory of her mother, was gone. And it was all her fault.

"Rollo!" she screamed, running up toward the caves, where she knew her brother was playing. "Rollo!"

Alerted by her desperate shouting, he was already making his way down to the inlet. "What is it?" he called.

Asa beckoned with both arms. "We have to go! Aboard *Northseeker*! Quickly!"

Rollo was running now and Asa hurried down to the edge of the water. Two dozen colored stones, piled in a pyramid, marked where the gangplank of *Northseeker* waited. The ship was invisible to all but those upon it. Asa didn't hesitate but stepped into space and found herself on the wooden plank. Rollo had finally caught up as she was winding in the anchor.

"What's happened?" he panted.

"I had the Moonstone Star. Tide stealers came."

His eyes turned to circles. "No! They took it?"

"Ten seconds ago."

"I'll go in."

"Rollo, no!"

"Breath of a fish within me!" he called, then dived over the edge of the ship and into the water.

Asa and her brother had been enchanted so that

he could breathe underwater and she could turn into a raven. But the magic made them sick if they used it. Asa didn't want Rollo to get sick, and she worried about him when he disappeared into the murky depths. She waited on *Northseeker,* tapping her fingers on the gunwales anxiously as she watched the water.

Under the water, it was cloudy and dark. Rollo peered into the green gloom for any trace of the tide stealers' longship. The flash of an oar caught his eye, and he swam toward it. Through the seaweed he saw the stern of a ship, cutting rapidly toward a deep trench. It disappeared. They were moving too fast for him.

He shot up to the surface. In his enchanted state, he could see *Northseeker,* and Asa helped him aboard.

"They've disappeared through a trench," he said, panting. "If we sail straight out of the inlet, we might be able to catch them on the other side of the headland."

"Let's go," she said, and *Northseeker* began to move away from the shore.

"We should tell Aunt Katla," Rollo said, shaking

water out of his hair and wrapping a fur around his body for warmth.

"There's no time." Asa glanced over her shoulder. "We might have the Star back in a couple of hours. She'll never notice we're gone."

Rollo took a deep breath. "We have to get it back."

Asa's hand tightened on the tiller. What would they do when they found the tide stealers? These underwater outlaws were the most feared thieves in the entire sunken kingdom. Trained by Flood and given the magical ability to breathe underwater, they had turned on him and formed into gangs of pirates to plunder the riches of all the underwater towers and churches. She had never met one before, but the tales about them were fearsome. Had her magic spell attracted them? Or was it just the light of the Moonstone Star glistening in the water that had caught their attention? Either way, Asa felt guilty.

Northseeker was rounding the headland now and cutting through the water down into a misty cove.

"You think they went this way?" she said to Rollo.

"I'm certain."

In the distance, she could see the mouths of two caves. Rollo had spotted them, too.

"Tide stealers live in caves, don't they?" he said.

"Yes," she said.

"Does that mean . . . ?"

"Yes," she said again. "We have to go in there."

CHAPTER 2

CAVE OF GHOSTS

Rollo's stomach was already twitching and cramping by the time they approached the two caves. It was fun being able to breathe underwater and not feel the cold, but the sickness that came afterward was no fun at all. In fact, it felt like he was going to be sicker than the first time. He put on a brave face for Asa, who was glancing from one cave to the other.

"Which one?" she muttered under her breath. "Which one looks like tide stealers live in it?"

Rollo looked at the first cave, then the second. Both of them were only partially underwater, which would mean they were able to sail into them. Both of them were dark and shadowy, and both of them were veiled in fine mist. But the first cave had a bigger entrance.

"It must be that one," he said, pointing to it. "They have to get their longship in and at least seventeen men."

"That's what I thought," Asa said. "But I feel something . . ."

Rollo turned to look at her. She was frowning. "What can you feel?"

"Cold air."

"It is cold."

"No, like . . . like something bad and cold is in there and the cold is blowing out onto the water."

"Maybe there's a blowhole at the back."

"Maybe. Maybe it's ghosts."

Rollo felt a chill up his spine. Even though

Northseeker was invisible to the real world, it was visible to the spirit world. All kinds of ghosts and monsters could see it; and while they were aboard, they could see the ghosts and monsters. "Do you want to try the other cave?"

Asa's eyes darted to the smaller one. "No. I think you're right. They'll be in the larger one. And a blow-hole would explain the cold breeze." She turned the tiller, and *Northseeker* cruised under an overhanging rock toward the cave mouth.

"What are we going to do when we get there?" Rollo asked.

"We're going to ask for our Moonstone Star back."

"Is that it?" Rollo's stomach gurgled and he had to swallow hard. More than anything, he just wanted to lie down and curl up and wait for the nausea to pass.

"What else can we do?" Asa snapped. "We're children. Moonstone isn't precious, so maybe they'll say yes. That's if they don't know it's magic."

"How would they know it was magic?"

13

She shrugged.

He grew suspicious. "Asa, what were you doing with the Star down at the inlet?"

She shrugged again.

"Did Aunt Katla know you had it?"

"It's not Aunt Katla's, Rollo. It's mine."

"It's Mama's."

"Mama's not alive, so it's mine."

Rollo held his tongue. He refused to believe his parents were actually dead. "Still, Aunt Katla had it above the fireplace for safekeeping."

"I was experimenting a little. Mama always told me that the sea made the Star's magic work. I was trying a spell, to catch a fish."

"And you caught a shipful of tide stealers instead." Rollo pressed his arm to his sore stomach.

Asa reached out to touch his shoulder. "You're sick."

"Yes, I am."

"It's all my fault."

"Well, that makes a change," he said with a weak smile. "Usually it's all *my* fault."

"Lie down for a little while," she said, shrugging out of her fur cloak and placing it in the bottom of the boat. "I'll tell you when we're going to anchor."

Rollo lay down on his back but didn't close his eyes. He watched as the sky disappeared overhead and the roof of the cave came into view. The last of the light vanished behind them and *Northseeker*'s sails took on an eerie blue-gray glow.

Asa gasped.

"I see it," Rollo said. "*Northseeker* glows in the dark!"

The cobwebby sails fluttered in the cold breeze. The dim light was weak in the darkness and flickering shadows moved around them. The shifting and bobbing of the boat was making his stomach gurgle and heave. He struggled to his feet and just got to the side in time to vomit over the edge and into the black water.

Asa rubbed his back. "Are you all right?"

"It's much worse than last time," he said. "I think it must get worse every time we use our enchantments."

"Well, let's be more careful about how often we use them. Only as a last resort." She peered into the dark.

The cold air licked around them—much colder than it should've been in the cave protected from the wind. "Can you feel that?" she said.

"My skin's prickling." He shivered. "It's icy in here."

"I can't see any sign of tide stealers," she said nervously. "I don't hear voices."

"Maybe they're much deeper inside the cave."

"What was that?" Asa's head snapped around, her eyes tracking some invisible movement.

"I didn't see anything."

"Check inside the boxes," she said, nodding toward the storage boxes in the ship. "See if there's anything to light a torch. I don't like sailing into the dark."

Rollo swallowed down the taste of vomit and went to the boxes. By the weak blue-gray light, he searched inside and turned up a lantern and four long matches. He struck one against the side of the boat. It flared to life, and he held it to the wick of the lantern with a shaking hand.

"Give it to me," Asa whispered, and he put the lantern into her fingers.

She held it up high . . .

And screamed.

Rollo forgot his nausea. Above them, crowded onto ledges of rock, were ghosts. Dozens and dozens of ghosts.

They had long arms and vaporous tails instead of legs. They wore long grayish white cloaks and hoods that partly covered ghoulish faces: all teeth and holes for eyes. It appeared that they were asleep, curled against each other like a litter of puppies Rollo had once seen. But the glow of the lantern was bright, and some of them began to stir.

"Asa, the light. Blow it out!"

"Then we won't be able to see them."

Ghosts began to move and wake, their sightless eyes turning toward the lantern. A set of misty arms reached for *Northseeker*'s mainmast.

"Turn around," Rollo said. "We have to get out."

"I'm *trying* to turn around." She pulled hard on the tiller, but *Northseeker* moved slowly.

"What's happening?"

"I don't think there's room to turn around properly."

One of the ghosts had grasped the mainmast and was now slithering down, a streak of fog with long, spiny fingers and a twisted, eyeless face.

Rollo grabbed the lantern from Asa and ran to the bow of the ship. He held the light high, illuminating the way forward. "Asa, there's a bend ahead and room to turn around."

"How do we get this thing off our ship?"

"I don't know, but let's move quickly."

Northseeker, sensing their urgency, lurched and knocked the tiller out of Asa's hand. Long, groping fingers snatched at the masts. The first ghost still clung to *Northseeker,* its head lolling from side to side as it got its balance, and Rollo plowed through the open box, looking for a weapon to use against it. But he knew nothing about ghosts: could he hit them, or burn them, or knock them into the water?

Just as he'd thought, around the bend the cave opened out. Shadows flickered all around them. *Northseeker* slowed and turned. Rollo glanced up at the ghost on the mast again and realized that its horrible hollow eyes were focused on something, transfixed.

The lantern.

"Asa, I think it's attracted to the flame," he said.

"That would make sense," she replied. "It's dark in there. The lantern woke them up."

Rollo advanced toward the mast.

"What are you doing?" She panicked.

"Just keep steering," he said. "I think I know what to do."

He held the lantern aloft and the ghost's head turned to focus on it. He snapped the glass door of the lantern open. "Come on, ghost. Come a bit closer."

The ghost began to slither down the mast.

"Rollo, be careful!" Asa called.

"Come on. Come and see the pretty light."

The mist began to unravel from the mast and curl across the deck in Rollo's direction. His heart was pounding and an eerie coldness washed around him as the mist drew closer. A caress across the back of his knuckles made his skin shiver and his hair stand on end.

Then the ghost began to stream into the lantern, turning into a thin line and curling around the light. Rollo's hand trembled, but he held the lantern still. When the last cold tail of ghostly mist had disappeared inside the lantern, he clapped the door shut.

"We're about to pass under the ghosts again," Asa said.

The lantern began to rattle and shake.

"Quickly! This thing's getting angry."

"Go, *Northseeker*," Asa said.

Northseeker skimmed forward. The ghosts above them reached out their hands, and the lantern jumped in Rollo's fingers. A grim spirit with arms like snakes brushed its fingers on the mainmast.

Rollo threw the lantern.

Bang!

It split into pieces and the ghost poured out. A gust of icy air. Fire was twisted through the spectral mist and all the other ghosts shrank back from it. *Northseeker* slid past them quickly, and a moment later the first glimmer of daylight appeared ahead of them.

"We're going to make it," Rollo said. His stomach was gurgling again and all his limbs felt like lead. He dropped to the floor, clutching his abdomen.

The sky reappeared and Asa bent over him. "I guess we got the wrong cave."

He sat up. Already, *Northseeker* was heading for the other cave entrance in search of the tide stealers. "I wonder if tide stealers are harder to outrun than ghosts," he said grimly.

"Yes," she said. "I wonder."

CHAPTER 3
SKALTI WOLFKILLER

With their lantern destroyed, Rollo and Asa only had the faint glow of *Northseeker*'s sails to light their way into the second cave. But already it was evident that the tide stealers lived here. Their longship was anchored up ahead and a light glimmered deep inside the cave. Voices echoed down the tunnel toward them.

"Are we going to anchor?" Rollo asked.

Asa turned to look at him. By the dim light, he looked pale and shaken. He was still very sick.

"We can wait here a little while if you like. Until you're feeling better."

"I'm all right now. My stomach has settled." He pressed his hand to his belly. "I'm still tired and a bit queasy, but I don't think we should stay here too long. I'll think twice before using my enchantment again."

"Was it really that much worse than last time?"

He shrugged. "I think so. More violent, but getting better doesn't take as long."

She dropped the anchor. "We'll go from here on foot. Very quietly."

"We're just going to walk into their camp?"

"I don't think they'll hurt children. At least, I hope they won't." She lowered the gangplank. "No more talking now. Once we're off *Northseeker*, they might be able to hear us."

Rollo eased himself up and followed her down the gangplank. Asa helped him onto the gravelly shore and held his hand tightly. His fingers were cold. She waited a moment for her eyes to adjust to the dark, then pointed to the dim light. Rollo nodded and they set off.

One step, two. Then light and weight were upon them. Shouting voices. Big, hairy men with ropes.

"Catch them!"

"What are you doing here?"

Asa blinked into a bright lantern. Rough hands had her and were bending her arms behind her back.

"Rollo!" she cried.

"Asa," came the muffled reply.

Her hands were tied together. She heard the sounds of struggle and turned to see Rollo. He had almost gotten away, but a fat man with a filthy shirt punched him in the stomach and slung him over his shoulder.

"Let me go!" she screamed, kicking and struggling.

Another man, laughing at her efforts, grabbed her legs with ease and roped them together, too. He pulled the knots so tight that she could feel the rope cutting into her skin.

"Come on, little thieves," he said. "We're taking you to the Wolfkiller."

Asa twisted her head so she could see Rollo. He hung limply over the fat man's shoulder. She hated herself for having gotten them into this mess. Down a long corridor they traveled, and the lamplight cast grim shadows over the tide stealers' crooked faces. There were six of them in all and they stank of sweat and seaweed. Within a few minutes, they rounded the corner into a brightly lit room. The other tide stealers were all here, crowded around a fire where ten fish

hung on a spit, roasting. The smoke had nowhere to escape, so it clung to the ceiling of the cave. Asa coughed and heard Rollo coughing, too. Good—at least he wasn't dead.

At the head of the fire, sitting on a wooden chair, was a man with long yellow hair and a circlet of gold upon his forehead. He was dressed in the same filthy clothes as the others, but there was something about him that set him apart—his clear gaze, his straight back, the determined set of his lips as Asa and Rollo were dumped on the ground in front of him. Asa recognized him as the leader of the tide stealers, the one who had stolen the Star with his silver whip.

She lay there for a moment, looking up at him. Everyone grew silent; the only sound was the crack and pop of the fire. The man glanced at her, at Rollo, then said in a loud, clear voice, "You've brought me children?"

A nervous laugh chased itself around the cave. Asa struggled to sit up. "Please," she said, "the little moonstone you took from us—it's worth nothing to you, but it's our greatest treasure. It belonged to our mother."

Rollo chimed in. "It's our last memory of her."

The man stroked his chin. Asa noticed he wore a necklace of wolf teeth, and they rattled softly as he moved. "Your mother?"

"Can you untie us, please?" Rollo said. "You said yourself we're only children."

Asa glanced at Rollo and noticed his lip was split and blood was smeared on his chin.

"Yes," she said. "Rollo's only ten and he's been ill, and look what your men have done to him."

The man indicated that the children should be untied. He climbed down from his wooden chair and crouched in front of them. Asa rubbed her wrists and ankles.

"I am Skalti Wolfkiller," he said. "What are your names?"

"We just want our Star back," Rollo said.

"You won't tell me your names?"

Asa shook her head and pressed her lips together tightly.

Skalti Wolfkiller smiled and deep lines appeared around his eyes. "Then you have told me everything I need to know." He stood, beckoned with a tilt of his head. "Come. I need to speak with you away from my men."

Asa climbed to her feet and helped Rollo up. Some of the tide stealers were watching curiously, but most had turned back to the fire or begun to splash ale into their cups. Skalti led them to another cave that branched off from the first. Rollo held Asa's hand tightly. It was cold in the second cave, away from the fire. Skalti indicated they should sit on the moldy rushes on the ground, but the children stood where they were. He folded his arms over his chest and considered them in the dark.

"I know who you are," he said at last.

Asa didn't say a word. Rollo tightened his grip on her hand.

Skalti leaned forward, smiled, and dropped his voice to a whisper. "I knew your mother."

Asa could see out of the corner of her eye that Rollo

was trying to catch her gaze, but she didn't budge.

"We just want our Star back," she said.

"Well," Skalti said, starting to pace, "that might prove difficult."

"But it means nothing to you and it means everything to us!" Asa protested.

"I'd give it back if I had it," Skalti said. "I'm sorry."

"Who has it?" Rollo gasped.

Skalti didn't answer him. He stopped in front of Asa. "The way it shone in the water, we thought it was a Great Sea Diamond. But no, we got it on board and realized it was just a little piece of moonstone. So one of my men threw it over the side in disgust."

"Where?" Rollo said. "I'll go and get it."

Skalti held up a finger. "There's more. It happened in the trench. A sea giant saw it gleaming and caught it as we passed."

Asa gulped. Her throat had gone dry. "A sea giant has our Star?"

"It's not all bad news. I recognized this sea giant. He lives in a colony at Blackwing Towers, a group of

31

sunken towers just north of here." Skalti patted Rollo's shoulder. "I can give you directions."

Asa could have cried. Ghosts, tide stealers, and now sea giants?

"I see what you're thinking," Skalti said to her. "But sea giants are stupid and they all sleep after lunch. If you go now, you may be lucky. I'll make sure my men give you safe passage back to your ship." He smiled again. "Your *invisible* ship, Asa."

"We'll find our own way back," she said, tugging Rollo's hand.

"We have a common enemy, you and I," Skalti called behind them. "His name is Flood."

Asa said nothing. She knew that she and Rollo were each worth a thousand gold coins to whoever captured them and handed them over to Flood. So what if Skalti hated Flood as much as she and Rollo did? He was a tide stealer, and tide stealers were more interested in money than loyalty.

On board *Northseeker,* Rollo took the tiller while Asa checked the map.

"Here," she said, jabbing at it with her finger. "Blackwing Towers. Out of the cove and north."

"Let's hope they're all asleep," said Rollo as *Northseeker* sailed out into the daylight again.

CHAPTER 4

A STORM AT SEA

"Uh-oh." Asa looked at the sky and Rollo followed her gaze. Dark gray clouds were sweeping in from the south, piled high like huge breakers.

"I think it looks like a storm," she said. "Maybe we should go home and come back another day."

He shook his head. "It's probably just a bit of rain. Aunt Katla will never let us come out looking for sea giants."

"But, Rollo, you've been sick and—"

"I'm fine now," he said firmly. "I want our Moonstone Star back." He nodded at the map. "How far to Blackwing Towers?"

Asa traced the course with her fingers. "It might take us two hours to get there. But Blackwing Towers is big. There are five towers all together and it might take us all day to explore them. Perhaps we should—"

"No," Rollo said firmly. "We're not going home now. So far today we've avoided ghosts and escaped from a band of tide stealers. If we go home, Aunt Katla won't let us out again until we're grown up and we'll never get the Star back."

Asa glanced anxiously at the sky.

"Come on, Asa. I know we can do this. Skalti said the giants would all be asleep after lunch. We'll go in—"

"*You'll* have to go in. Underwater. Although you'll get sick again," Asa said.

"But then we'll be on our way home. We'll have the Star and Aunt Katla will be cross, but at least we'll have it back."

She looked to the sky again. "Maybe it is only rain," she said.

"Luck's on our side today." He nudged her. "I just know it."

With a brisk wind at their backs, within half an hour *Northseeker* was out of the cove and spearing northward. Rollo's stomach felt more settled and he began to think that the illness hadn't been so bad after all. Clouds moved in and grew darker. Asa was busy studying the map, so she didn't notice at first, and for that Rollo was glad. The bottom edge of the storm front was black and the wind was picking up. The sea beneath them was rolling restlessly. If she noticed, Rollo knew she might change her mind and make them go home.

But the first rumble of thunder got her attention.

"What was that?" she said, looking up from the map.

He shrugged, but she had seen the clouds, close on their tail.

"Oh no," she said. "It *is* a storm."

"It might just be rain," he said lamely, but a huge crack of thunder split the sky and there was no denying it anymore. They were stuck out on the open sea, with a huge storm bearing down on them.

Asa scanned the horizon desperately. "We have to get to cover."

"There's nothing."

"Then we have to go back."

"We'll sail straight into the storm." Rollo looked up at *Northseeker*'s sails. They flapped madly against the darkening sky. "No, we're going to have to roll up the sails and ride it out."

"Why roll them up?" she asked. "They don't run on wind; they run on magic."

"But the wind's so strong it might tear them."

As if to prove his point, a stiff gust tore a thin stream of cobweb sail loose and sent it dashing into the sky.

Rollo wrapped his arms around the smaller mast and pulled himself up. His knees clenched the timber

tightly. It wasn't much different from climbing a tree. He got a foothold on a notch in the wood and pulled himself up.

"Careful, Rollo," Asa said, but her words were torn out of her mouth by the wind.

He shinnied up a little farther. The silver rope that kept the sails fastened was in reach. He jerked it loose and then used it to pull himself higher. Working quickly, he furled the sails gently and tied them down.

Then he slid down the mast. "That was fun," he said, turning to the mainmast.

"Hurry, the wind's picking up," Asa said.

Rollo began to climb again. This mast was higher and the wind was growing more intense. He concentrated hard. The boat was pitching this way and that, heaving up over waves, then dropping into hollows. He was near the yardarm now and the sails hanging from it flapped wildly. He began to roll them up.

"Hurry!" Asa called.

The first fat drop of rain fell on his hand. He worked fast. A sudden gust of squally wind sent the boat lurching violently. The mast tipped and he clung on as hard as he could.

"Come down!" Asa yelled above the wind.

He tied the last knot and slid back down the mast. She grabbed him and pulled him onto the deck next to her. They curled up as tight as they could under the seat, but the rain was hard and the wind blew it diagonally. Soon they were soaked. *Northseeker* pitched violently and Asa closed her eyes in terror. Rollo felt guilty. It was all right for him to be out here in the storm: if *Northseeker* sank, he would be safe in the water. Asa could drown.

"It'll be all right," he said to her over the sound of the rain and the wind.

At that precise moment, a blinding flash split the sky overhead and the metallic crack of thunder rang all around them. Rollo peered out from under the seat. *Northseeker's* mainmast had been hit by lightning. It was on fire!

Asa scrambled out of her hiding place. "No!" she cried.

Rollo was right behind her. "Will the rain put it out?"

"The fire's moving too fast."

The sky was almost black with cloud, as though nighttime had come in the middle of the day. Against the dark sky, the fire was bright yellow. Fat raindrops hissed and smoldered, but the fire didn't go out. It burned, slow but stubborn.

"I'll have to go up again," Rollo said. He raced to the mast and began to climb.

Northseeker rolled and Rollo tried to keep his balance. From up here, he could see that they were being pulled off course. Strong currents of air and water from the storm dragged the ship away with them. But he couldn't think about that now; he had to put the fire out.

It was licking down toward the yardarm. He drew as close as he could to the flames, holding on so hard with his knees that they ached. His fur coat was soaked, so he dragged it off and threw it over the fire. Missed. It went flying over and back down. He caught the edge of it and hauled it up again. Threw it. This time it caught and hung there in the rain. The fire was smothered.

Rollo allowed himself to slide down the mast again. The rain was easing and the wind dying down. Asa waited in the cold, wet air. Her face was pale and anxious.

"Let's get back under the seat," she said.

Once again they sheltered from the storm. It raged and rumbled all around them, fading slowly from black to gray. When the worst of it seemed to have passed, she peered out.

"I don't see sun."

"I see a patch of blue sky," Rollo said, pointing behind them.

Asa scanned the horizon. "Where on earth are we?"

Rollo shook his head. "*Northseeker,* take us north."

To his surprise, the ship shook her own sails free and began to move.

Asa laughed. "Well, that saves you another trip up the mast."

"I'm getting quite good at it."

But already she was growing serious again, consulting her maps. "As soon as we see a landmark, I'll know where we are and can plot a course back."

"I hope it's not too far. Skalti said the giants sleep after lunch, but how long do you think they sleep? An hour or two?"

"More importantly, what do they eat for lunch?" she added with a lift of her dark eyebrows. "Let's hope it's not children."

CHAPTER 5

THE LAIR OF THE SEA GIANTS

The shadows of *Northseeker*'s masts were growing long across the deck when they finally spotted a landmark. A black spire poked out of the water, long and elegant and decorated with a bird in flight.

Asa scanned her map. "I can't see anything like this," she said.

"Let me look," said Rollo, and Asa handed him the map. "We could still be miles from—"

"Here we are," he said, pointing to a spot on the map.

She turned back to him. He could see the surprise in her face. She didn't usually make mistakes.

"Where? Are we close to Blackwing Towers?"

"Asa, this *is* Blackwing Towers."

She leaned over the side of the ship, and he joined her. They were skimming through the water past the spire now, looking down into the drowned turrets of an old castle.

"One . . . two . . . three . . . four . . . five . . . ," she said as she counted the towers beneath them.

"There are so many! How will we know which one the giants live in?"

"This must have been the biggest castle in the Star Lands."

"No, I remember Papa telling me that Castle Crag had eleven towers."

She shuddered. "Castle Crag."

"Flood's castle," he said. "The only one that didn't go under."

"I hate him, Rollo," Asa said, her dark eyes narrowing.

"Mama always said it doesn't pay to hate anyone."

"Well, I hate Flood," she said, taking the tiller and easing them past the final tower. "If it weren't for him, we wouldn't be soaking wet and far from home and about to take on a colony of sea giants. Stop, *Northseeker*."

The longship slowed and stopped, right in the center, between the five towers.

"Which one?" Rollo said, gazing across the water.

"This is too hard. What if it's in the last one you look at? You'll just keep getting sicker and sicker."

"Not if I don't get out of the water," he said. "I'll stay under the enchantment until I've got the Star back."

"Are you sure you won't be cold?"

"I don't feel the cold when I'm breathing like a fish," he said.

Asa peered into the water. "Be careful."

"I'm just going to have a look. I'll come and tell you if I spot a giant." He glanced up at the sky. The clouds had dispersed and the sun was dipping lower. What if all the giants were awake again? He summoned up every bit of courage he had. "Breath of a fish within me!" he said, and dived into the sea.

The water was clear here and the dark towers were lit up by spears of sunlight. Rollo swam down a little way and found a window encrusted with barnacles. He pried it open and swam through.

Rollo found himself in a large, round room. Chairs and cushions and plates and cups were all jumbled up against the wall, where they had sat since the flood swept them away. Swollen books had fallen from stone shelves and now grew green algae on the floor. Rollo couldn't see any sign of giants. He swam through the doorway and into a hall, checked up and down, then moved slowly toward another doorway. The muffled sounds of the sea and the bubbles of his own breath were the only noises he could hear. He swam into another room. A huge wing-backed chair had fallen over on its side. He moved toward it and thought he saw someone gray and gaunt behind

it. His heart skipped a beat. He paddled backward rapidly, then reassessed what he was seeing. The light was dim, the water playing tricks on his eyes. Surely this was just a bunch of old sticks. He swam closer to investigate.

A skeleton!

Rollo recoiled. He had never seen a dead person before. Until Flood performed his awful magic, Rollo had lived a quiet and happy life. Now he knew all kinds of horrors. He wondered if the skeleton had been lying there since the flood, or if it was the remains of the last person who had taken on the sea giants. He backed off quickly, out into the hallway and through the first window. He swam down and found another opening. This time he didn't go in but stuck his head through for another look around. More jumbled furniture and strange objects. No sign that giants had ever lived here.

Below him the sea grew dark: too dark to investigate, but also too dark for sea giants—who had notoriously bad eyesight—to live. This wasn't the right tower. He turned his gaze upward to *Northseeker.* He swam up and touched the side, found Asa peering anxiously down at him.

"Find anything?"

Rollo decided not to tell her about the skeleton. "No," he said.

"I've been thinking," she said. "The tower with the spire. The first one we passed . . ."

"You think they're in that one?"

"It would make sense. The first one they'd go to because it's easy to find."

"I'll meet you over there." Down he went again, before the enchantment wore off. He swam quickly, shooting down through the water to an open window in the new tower. He found an empty room. Out in the hall, he spotted a doorway leading to a bigger room. He hesitated. He could see shapes in there, big, pale shapes. They weren't moving.

Be brave, he told himself, and swam toward the door. He paused and peered around.

A room full of sleeping sea giants.

They looked sort of like normal people, except they

were nine feet tall and had thick, bony foreheads. Their hands were large and their fingers were all as stumpy and clumsy as thumbs. Because they lived under the water, they had scaly skin, and some had fins instead of feet.

He didn't dare go into the room, but examined them from the doorway, his eyes moving from one to the next. They sat in a circle, leaning on each other, their chests rising and falling peacefully as they slept. Suddenly he spotted it. A faint white glow: the Moonstone Star hung around the neck of a big, ugly, fin-footed giant.

Swimming quickly, he moved back out of the tower and up toward *Northseeker*. He swam up the side of the tower and followed the turret to the spire. The carved bird on the spire gave him an idea.

"I found them," he said to Asa as he burst out of the water.

"Are there many?"

"About seven. We don't have much time; I have to get back under before the enchantment wears off. One of them is wearing the Star around his neck. I'm going to wake him up and I'm going to get him to chase me up here so you can get the Star."

"How am I supposed to do that? He'll see me. He'll try to catch me."

"Not if you're a bird," Rollo said, nodding at the bird on the spire. "He won't expect it."

She took a deep breath. "But what if—"

His lungs started to feel dry. "I have to go," he said, quickly bobbing under the water. Just in time. The enchantment stayed on him. He swam down again, through the window, worrying that he hadn't explained himself clearly enough to Asa. What if she didn't realize he meant for her to change into a bird? As a raven, she could surprise the giant, pluck the Star off him, and head back to *Northseeker* before he'd even realized his treasure was missing. He came once again to the room where the giants were sleeping. Slowly, he swam through. All at once, it seemed so easy. Not one of them had even stirred. The Star was just there, waiting. All he had to do was grab it and swim fast. Maybe he wouldn't have to rely on Asa at all. . . .

Boldly, he reached down and seized the Star to pull it. At the same moment, a massive, crushingly strong hand snapped around his wrist.

The giant was awake and glaring at him with blood-shot eyes. His voice hissed and bubbled under the water. "What do you think you're doing, puppy?"

CHAPTER 6
A COMMON ENEMY

Asa steeled herself. As soon as Rollo appeared, she would turn into a raven and circle the spire until the giant came up. Grab the Star in her beak, distract the giant long enough for Rollo to get away, and fly back to *Northseeker.* It seemed risky, and she had the feeling that perhaps this whole adventure had been a mistake. Perhaps she should have gone home, confessed to Katla that she had lost the Moonstone

Star, and left it at that. They had lost so much else.

Half an hour passed. She grew worried.

Another half hour. Now she was frantic.

Carefully, she climbed over the side of the ship and took a deep breath. As she slid into the water, the salt stung her eyes. She swam a few feet from the boat but couldn't see anything. Her breath grew hard in her lungs. She swam back and climbed aboard again. Now she was cold and wet and frantic.

Something had gone wrong.

What was she to do? She fixed her eyes on the spire again, willing the sun to stay up a little longer. Already the sky was flushing pink and the sea caught the milky reflection.

A bubbling noise behind her drew her attention. She spun around, in time to see the tide stealers' ship surging out of the water.

"Not again," she muttered, holding still. They wouldn't be able to see *Northseeker,* but it frightened her nonetheless, especially when she was so on edge about Rollo.

To her surprise, the ship surfaced with only one man aboard. Skalti Wolfkiller. He searched the horizon with his eyes, then he placed a hand on either side of his mouth and called, "Asa! Rollo!"

Asa froze. He was looking for them. He knew their names, he knew who they were, and he was looking for them.

"Asa! Rollo! Show yourselves, children. I don't want to hurt you. I want to help."

Asa stood still and held her breath, even though she knew he couldn't see her.

"I saw the storm blow in and I was worried about you. Sea giants are dangerous. You need my help." He turned in a slow circle, searching all around him. "I know you're here somewhere," he shouted. "Don't be fools, let me help you."

Asa's heart thundered. Rollo was nowhere in sight and she had run out of ideas. And here was a tide stealer, armed with swords and knives and huge, bulging muscles, offering to help.

"Trust me, children. I knew your mother. Before

I became what I am now, I was one of her footmen. I bear Flood no love. I won't betray you."

Asa flipped open the lid of the box and pulled out an empty metal biscuit tin. She tossed it gently into the water. It splashed and began to sink. Skalti's head snapped around. He smiled in relief. "I'm coming," he said, and dived into the water.

As he swam toward her, Asa leaned over the side with her hand ready to pull him to the boat. Within a few moments, his big, hard hands were nearby. She grabbed his wrist and pulled him.

He hit the side of the boat and looked up at her. "There you are."

"I don't trust you," she said in a serious voice. "If you make one wrong move, I'll turn into a bird and fly away."

"I will earn your trust, Princess Asa," he said, and heaved himself up the side of the ship. He stood, dripping wet, and looked around. "A fine ship. A miniature of your father's own longship."

"*Northseeker,*" Asa said, keeping a wary distance.

"And where is your brother?"

Her eyes flicked momentarily to the spire, then back to Skalti. "Under the water. He was supposed to get a sea giant to chase him back up here, but—"

Skalti set his mouth in a hard line. "A dangerous plan."

"I know. But some things are too important to lose."

"Your parents will be proud of you if they hear of it."

Asa frowned. "Don't you know? My parents are dead."

"Are they?" His face was puzzled. "Ah, I suppose they are. Flood would be foolish not to have killed them. It's just that I heard . . ."

"What have you heard?"

"Ragni is still alive, so I assumed your parents were also. You know who Ragni is, don't you?"

"Yes. The secret court sorcerer. The one who gave us our enchantments. He's alive?"

"In a way. Flood spared him, at a terrible cost." Skalti shook his head. "We waste too much time with all this talking. How long has your brother been gone?"

"Nearly an hour." She glanced up at the sky. "Night is coming."

He nodded with an air of finality. "I'll go after him. You wait here."

Asa took a deep breath. "Please find him."

"I'll do my best."

After Fin-foot the giant grabbed Rollo's hand, there were a few minutes of confusion. Rollo was seized, tied, and dragged around. Other sea giants woke up and prodded him, licked their lips, congratulated the giant on his catch. He struggled against his bonds but couldn't get free. How long would it take Asa to figure out he had been captured? And what could she do, anyway?

The sea giants took him to a large room with an empty fireplace. There was no furniture. They tied a rock to his ankles and left him. Piled by the fireplace was an assortment of large pots and knives and nets, and he presumed this was the kitchen. Why had they brought him to the kitchen? Unless—no—did they intend to . . . *eat him*?

Panicking, Rollo kicked and squirmed.

A bubbling noise behind him alerted him to the fact that one of the sea giants had returned. He waited, absolutely still, and watched. This one looked like a woman with long, stringy hair and an apron frilled with seaweed. She swam to the fireplace and, to Rollo's astonishment, lit a fire.

"How did you do that?" he asked.

She turned and looked at him. "Do what?"

"Light a fire underwater?"

"Sea fire," she said. "Giants' magic." Then she shook her head. "Why am I talking to dinner?" She hefted one of the big pots onto a hook over the fire and left.

Dinner. He had to get out of here.

He was alone again. Dragging the rock behind him, he squirmed through the water across to where the pots and knives and nets were stacked. If he could just get hold of one of those knives, he could cut the rope around his hands and get himself free. Rollo eyed the fire warily. The heat was radiating out into the room. Inch by inch, he wriggled and rolled his way across to the stack of kitchen implements. He struggled into a sitting position and shuffled up so that his hands, which were behind his back, could grasp the handle of a big knife.

Slowly, watching the door for movement, he began to rub the ropes around his wrists on the blade of the knife.

"Oh, no you don't!" A shadow appeared at the door, Fin-foot himself with the Moonstone Star around his neck.

Rollo could have cried! Fin-foot marched in, picked him up, and dragged him to the other corner of the room. For good measure, he tied another heavy rock to Rollo's feet.

Then he leaned over Rollo with a horrible grin. "You'll meet the knives soon enough," he said. "Because you won't fit in that pot otherwise."

Then he left.

Rollo's heart was thundering. He refused to accept

that he was going to be cut up and eaten by sea giants. As soon as Fin-foot was gone, he started struggling again, but the weights were too heavy this time. A shadow crossed the doorway and he glanced up, expecting another sea giant.

It was Skalti Wolfkiller.

Skalti held a finger to his lips and lunged forward, in one swift movement cutting the ropes at Rollo's ankles with his sword. Then he released Rollo's hand and grasped him under the armpit.

"Quickly," Skalti said. "Your sister is waiting for you."

Rollo's relief at being rescued was immediately tempered by disappointment that he hadn't stolen the Star. "But the Moonstone Star—" he started. But before he could finish his sentence, Fin-foot and two other sea giants burst into the room.

Skalti pushed him toward the window. "Go!" he said. "I'll take them."

Rollo swam quickly for the window. The shutters were closed and locked tight. He pushed, but they

wouldn't budge. He glanced over his shoulder. Skalti had pulled out his gleaming sword again and was hacking at the sea giants. Fin-foot darted out of the sword's arc and started in Rollo's direction.

"Move!" Rollo said to one of the shutters. He turned and put his feet against it, kicking hard. It creaked. A crack appeared. He kicked again. The weight of the water was holding it back, but the wood was saturated and starting to rot. He concentrated all his energy into his feet and kicked again. The shutter splintered and he glanced over his shoulder. One of the other giants had taken hold of a knife and was closing in on Skalti. Rollo squeezed through the hole in the shutter. Behind him, he heard the sound of wood splitting as Fin-foot forced himself through, too.

Rollo swam, faster than he'd ever swum. Up, up to the light and air, with Fin-foot on his tail.

CHAPTER 7

FIN-FOOT
THE SEA GIANT

Up on the surface, Asa waited as night closed in. The sun had disappeared and left only streaks of pale pink in its wake. She wondered if Skalti had found Rollo by now, and she also wondered if he only wanted to find him to sell him off to Flood. How she wished she'd never taken the Moonstone Star down from its place on the mantelpiece. It was the stupidest thing she'd ever done.

Her eyes turned back to the spire, the carved bird

on it with its black wings spread. Soon it would be so dark she wouldn't be able to see it at all.

Suddenly there was a rushing sound and Rollo's head popped out of the water.

"Rollo!" she cried joyfully.

"Bird, Asa!" he said, climbing up the spire. A moment later, behind him came a sea giant. His huge hands snatched at Rollo, but he was too slow to catch him. A glimmer of light at the giant's neck caught her eye: the Moonstone Star.

Asa spread her arms. "Wings of a raven upon me!"

Her body trembled, grew lighter. She could feel bones bending, her heart shrinking. Then her wings took her to the sky.

She circled quickly, getting her bearings. The sea giant had grabbed Rollo's shirt and was tugging him back into the water.

Asa dived, straight for the giant's face. As she flapped and clawed, the giant let Rollo go, and her brother splashed into the water and began to swim for *Northseeker.*

"Stupid bird!" the sea giant shouted, batting her away from him with his big hands.

But Asa wasn't finished yet. She darted off, then straight back, her beak aiming for the Moonstone Star.

The giant wasn't expecting it. He put his hands up to cover his face. She felt the Star in her beak, pulled hard. It came free.

"No!" shouted the giant. "Not my pretty!"

He reached out with his meaty fists, but it was too late. Asa had taken to the sky again. Joy and relief surged through her veins. She landed on *Northseeker* and pulled her own body back around her. She felt heavy and exhausted. The Star fell out of her mouth and onto the deck.

"We got away," she said, picking up the Star and tying it firmly around her neck.

"We didn't," Rollo replied quickly, pointing at the giant who was now swimming toward them.

"Of course," said Asa. "He can see the ship. He's a spirit of the deep. We're not invisible to him!"

"Then we'd better sail away—and quick."

Northseeker took the hint and sped forward. They would easily outrun the giant.

But then Skalti bobbed out of the water. His face was covered in blood and he was paddling madly toward his ship. The giant saw him and changed course.

"He's going to catch Skalti," Rollo cried.

"If we go back, he might catch us, too," Asa said.

"He saved my life."

Asa pulled on the tiller. "Quickly, *Northseeker*," she said. On one side was Skalti swimming for his ship; on the other, the giant swimming toward Skalti. *Northseeker* would pass between them: who would they intercept first?

Now that they were closer, Asa could see that Skalti's shoulder was bleeding. He could barely swim.

"Go, *Northseeker*," Rollo said, tapping the side of the boat. "We must get there before the giant does."

Northseeker cut a furrow through the silver water. The first stars had begun to glimmer in the sky, but it was hard to see where the ship was going. The giant roared and Asa's stomach turned to water.

"Nearly there . . . ," Rollo said.

"Skalti can't see us," she cried. "Throw something in the water."

Rollo picked a stone out of his pocket and cast it over the side.

Skalti saw it and guessed what they were doing. "No, go back!" he called. "I'll be all right."

Asa tore off her cloak and hurled it into the water ahead of them. It floated on the surface. Skalti realized they were not going to do as he said and he began to swim toward it. As the giant was closing in, *Northseeker* slowed next to the floating cloak and, obviously struggling, Skalti reached for it. The giant was three feet away, grabbing at them with meaty hands.

Skalti caught the outer edge of the cloak and the children caught the other end. They dragged him toward the ship.

"Quickly, now," Asa said as Skalti climbed aboard.

The giant's fingers brushed the stern and *Northseeker* leapt forward out of his reach. The ship skimmed away swiftly.

"We lost him!" Rollo cried.

Asa turned to Skalti. A deep cut in his shoulder oozed blood. His face was bruised and his nose was bleeding. "You're injured."

"Just take me back to my ship."

"We'll do better than that. We'll take you back to my aunt. She's very good at healing."

"But—"

Asa held a finger to her lips. "You saved us. Let us save you."

Every cloud had fled the sky and the moon was a bright orb above them as they sailed back to Two Hills Keep.

Rollo and Asa were both sick. Asa felt as though she had been trampled on by an entire colony of sea giants. Rollo had been right. It was much worse than the first time she had used her enchantment. Rollo barely lifted his head except to throw up over the side of the ship. Asa cleaned Skalti's wounds as best as she could, then

73

sat, exhausted and sore, at the tiller, guiding *Northseeker* home.

They anchored and dragged themselves up the hill. Asa feared Katla's anger but hoped that her aunt would still be kind to Skalti. One thing that she was sure of, though, was this: she was never letting go of the Moonstone Star again. She wasn't even going to let Katla hang it above the fireplace. It was going to stay on the ribbon around her neck.

Katla burst out the front door when she heard their voices. Her face looked like a thundercloud.

"Where have you *been*?" she demanded. Then her furious eyes lit on Skalti staggering limply behind them, and she softened.

"Aunty Katla," Asa said, "this man was injured saving our lives. Can you help him?"

Katla bustled them all inside, and Asa explained what had happened while her aunt went through her medicine cabinet looking for creams, herbs, and bandages. Within an hour, Skalti was sitting by the fire eating soup, while little Una played with a doll by his feet. Asa and Rollo, however, were dispatched off to bed without supper.

They were both too sick to eat, anyway.

"When are we going to tell Aunt Katla that Skalti is a tide stealer?" asked Rollo.

Asa had carefully left that detail out. "Tomorrow. When she's in a better mood." She snuggled down into bed, willing sleep to come quickly to her tired and aching body. Her joints felt hot and swollen and stiff.

Silence settled on the room, but then Rollo said, "I've been thinking . . ."

"About what?"

"About the Moonstone Star."

"Yes?" Asa touched it softly.

"You tried to make it send you a fish? This morning?"

"Yes, but it didn't work."

"But it should have. If Mama's dead, then you're the Star Queen."

She held her breath. "Yes, it should have. . . ."

"So maybe Mama's not dead."

She thought about Skalti and the fact that he hadn't been sure whether her mother was dead. He knew that Ragni, her father's secret magician, was still alive somewhere. Maybe . . . maybe . . .

No, she wouldn't tell Rollo. She didn't want to get his hopes up. Because she was young and untrained, the Star didn't work for her. Maybe when she was older and wiser, but not now.

"What do you think, Asa?" Rollo said.

"I think it's time to sleep," she said.

"But what if—"

"Rollo," she said sternly, "it won't do us any good to think about these things. Flood killed Mama and Papa a year ago. I miss them, but I'm starting to accept it. Maybe it's time you did, too."

"But don't you think there's even a possibility that they're still alive?"

A clock ticked quietly in the room. The fire crackled softly. Asa closed her eyes and remembered her mother's face, her father's hands. Ragni would know whether her parents were still alive. But she didn't know how she would find Ragni.

So she said nothing.

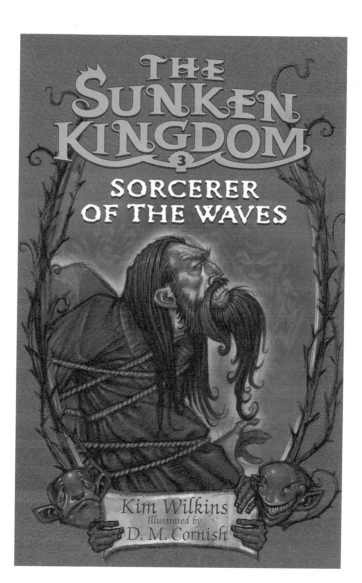

THE SUNKEN KINGDOM 3

SORCERER OF THE WAVES

Kim Wilkins

Illustrated by
D. M. Cornish

Asa and Rollo's adventures continue in . . .

THE SUNKEN KINGDOM
BOOK THREE

SORCERER
OF THE WAVES

"No!" Asa cried, pulling the tiller as much as she could.

Rollo joined her, resting his hand over hers and pulling hard. "Come on, *Northseeker,* let's go," he said.

Northseeker strained against the currents that tugged the ship beneath them. Then its prow began to dip. The mist parted suddenly and the children saw the whirlpool with frightening clarity. A deep funnel into the black water, half a mile across, its outer edge just a few yards ahead. And they were being dragged rapidly toward it.

ABOUT THE AUTHOR

Since the publication of her first novel, *The Infernal,* in 1997, Kim Wilkins has established herself as a leading fantasy author in Australia and internationally. Her books include *Grimoire*, *The Resurrectionists*, *Angel of Ruin*, *The Autumn Castle,* and *Giants of the Frost.* She has also written a series for young adults about a psychic detective. She lives in Brisbane, Australia.

Kim's first novel, *The Infernal,* won both the horror and fantasy novel categories of the Aurealis Awards in 1997.

ABOUT THE ILLUSTRATOR

After graduating from the University of South Australia, David Cornish took his portfolio to Sydney, where he found work with several magazines and newspapers. Three years later, an opportunity arose there to be on the drawing team of the game show *Burgo's Catchphrase*. After six years with the show, David became restless, circum-navigating the globe before returning to Adelaide, Australia.

David's bold, graphic style and fine draftsmanship have made him a successful illustrator in Australia, and in the United States he is best known as both the author and the illustrator of the fantasy series Monster Blood Tattoo.

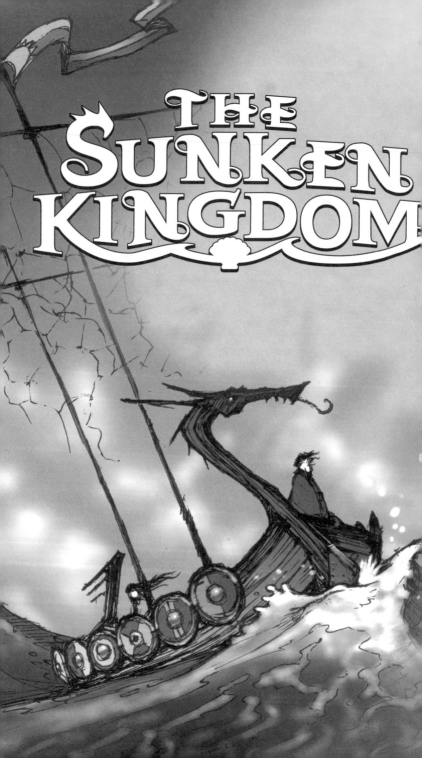